Meet The Author — Hazel Townson

What is your favourite animal?
An Alsatian dog
What is your favourite boy's name?
Christopher
What is your favourite girl's name?
Catherine
What is your favourite food?
Strawberries
What is your favourite music?
Classical, especially Mahler
What is your favourite hobby?
Table tennis

Meet The Illustrator — Martin Salisbury

What is your favourite animal?
Any wild cat
What is your favourite boy's name?
Charles
What is your favourite girl's name?
Stella
What is your favourite food?
Sausages and mash
What is your favourite music?
Patsy Cline
What is your favourite hobby?
Collecting illustrated books

D1392057

For my super son-in-law
Stuart Atherden

Contents

Chapter 1
The Iron Key

Adam Belman was bored. He had just moved to Hope School in the middle of term. The work was far less interesting than at his old school. The teachers here talked too much and there was nothing to do.

They were learning about the Second World War, which he found really boring. In fact, he was half-asleep in the middle of the lesson. He was thinking about nothing much when, all at once, he had an idea. He woke up with a jump. He just might have found the first clue to a puzzle!

Jade Green was the only person in his class who had shown any interest in him. She had told him that there was a secret room somewhere in the school. No-one had ever been able to find it.

Because he had nothing better to do, Adam had spent his free time going round the school looking for a hidden door. Perhaps if he found the secret room it would win him some friends.

Sadly he hadn't found any clues ... until now. In the middle of this boring lesson, he had an exciting idea.

The teacher, Mr Evans, had put a huge, old key on his table. The label hung over the table edge so that Adam could read it.

STOCK CUPBOARD. The label could be Adam's first clue, for no stock cupboard ever needed a key as big and as old as this one. And Hope School had just been done up. That label could not be the right one. It must be code for something else – like a secret room!

Adam Belman was wide awake now. His mind was racing. He must get hold of that key and begin to look into this at once.

3

Adam didn't hear a word of the lesson. At the end Mr Evans asked him to stay behind. This was Adam's great chance. He pretended to need some help. He leaned across the teacher's table and slipped the key into his pocket.

There was a staff meeting that day after school. Adam could try out the key while the teachers were busy. The only bad thing that could happen was that Mrs Yates, the caretaker, might see him. In that case he would tell her he'd been sent to look for his lost P.E. outfit and didn't dare go home without it.

After school, Adam hid himself in the toilets for a bit. Then he crept past the staffroom door to make sure that the meeting had begun. Yes, he could hear people talking and the chink of teacups.

Feeling safe, Adam went off to find the stock cupboard, which he knew was in a dark corner off the main hall. This end of the hall had a dusty, brown curtain in front of it. The folding dinner tables were kept behind it, with all the football gear and P.E. apparatus. In fact it was quite hard to get to the cupboard door at the back.

There was a huge keyhole in the door. The big key fitted it nicely. Adam looked back to make sure no-one was watching. Then he turned the key and opened the door. A light came on in the small room and he walked in.

He saw just what you would expect to see in a stock cupboard. There were shelves with pens, notebooks and class sets of readers. There were boxes of tissues and rulers and bundles of biros in boxes. Nothing odd here! There wasn't another door in the wall and there was no secret panel. Bad luck!

Ah, well! It had been a good idea to try. Perhaps he'd keep the key for a bit and see if it fitted somewhere else.

He was just about to leave when the door slammed shut behind him. The light went out. Then a key turned in the lock. Mrs Yates must have seen the door was open and locked it with her own key. What a good thing Adam hadn't left his key in the door. It was still safe in his hand! No need to panic. Adam waited a moment to give Mrs Yates time to go away. Then, feeling around in the dark, he found the keyhole and opened the door again. But now he did panic.

All the clutter behind the dusty, brown curtain had gone. The curtain had gone too. Year 6's art display, "In the Style of Monet",

which had been hanging on the walls of the hall, had gone too. All that was left on the walls were two posters from a long time ago. One said "Dig for Victory" and the other "Careless Talk Costs Lives".

Adam stared, shocked and amazed. He began to notice other changes. Every window now had thick, black curtains instead of pretty, flowery ones. All the panes of glass were criss-crossed with strips of brown sticky tape.

No-one could have made all these changes in the short time Adam had been in the cupboard. Something very odd was happening – something very scary.

Had he found the secret room after all?

Chapter 2
A Siren Sounds

Adam just stood there. He could not decide what to do. Should he step back into the cupboard at once, and hope to get back to where he'd come from? Or should he be brave and explore this weird and puzzling place which was both the same as the school hall, and yet quite different? This was his big chance. He was sure to have a stunning tale to tell. Everyone would want to hear it.

Before he could decide what to do, a girl ran into the hall. She saw him and called out, "Hurry up! The siren's gone! Didn't you hear it?"

He was pleased to see that it was Jade Green. She was running off somewhere very fast, carrying a coat and a cardboard box. For some odd reason, Jade wasn't wearing her school uniform. She had on a shabby dress and cardigan.

Adam had never heard a siren before. When it went off, he thought it was the fire alarm. He didn't know what to do. Jade grabbed his arm and dragged him off into the playground.

Neat lines of children were marching away from the school, across the playing field and down some steps into some concrete shelters. Adam had never noticed these before. None of the children wore

uniform. They all carried a coat and a cardboard box like Jade's.

Adam and Jade joined the end of one of the lines. They were soon sitting in a shelter with 30 other children and two teachers. They sat on wooden benches in the cold, damp dug-out. The floor was just soft earth. The teachers were holding up lamps and checking that the children were all there.

"Put your coats on! It's cold down here," ordered one teacher. The other asked Adam, "Where's your gas mask?"

"It's all right, sir, it's here!" Jade said. She pulled out something from under the bench and put it on Adam's lap. It was a cardboard box on a string, like the one she and all the others were holding.

"Well, keep it with you," said the teacher. "Don't put it down where you might lose it."

"Now remember not to ask for biscuits or water until we've been here at least half an hour," she went on. "And, Jade, I think it's your turn today to start the sing-song."

The children started with a song Adam didn't know (something about bluebirds over the white cliffs of Dover). He looked around him. He saw that one of the boys had a huge bottle of water and some paper cups, and a girl was holding a large tin of biscuits. Were they going to stay here all night? And if so, was this the only food and drink they'd get?

Adam shivered. He didn't like it down here. It smelt damp and nasty and the wooden bench was hard. "How long are we here for?" he asked Jade between songs.

"Until the 'All Clear', of course."

"When will that be?" asked Adam.

"Who knows?" said Jade. "Anyway, it's not all bad. We've missed the spelling test now."

Adam hadn't known about the spelling test, but anyway school must be over for the day. He looked at his watch. It had stopped at 3.45 pm, the time he'd gone into the cupboard.

None of this made any sense, but as long as Jade was there he felt everything would be all right in the end. He hadn't got used to this strange new school yet, but Jade had been here all her life. She would look after him.

Then the droning noises in the air above them turned into one great crash-bang.

Adam put his hands over his ears. Even down here, deep in this concrete bunker, he could feel the earth shaking all around him. It was weird. Everyone looked tense. Two girls were hugging each other and one of the boys began to cry. A teacher put an arm round him.

What was all this about? What had exploded so loudly? Then Adam understood that there was an air raid going on out there. Now he was really scared. He gripped Jade's arm, but she grinned and said, "It's OK, that one didn't sound too close."

At last, after more thuds and bangs, a long wail from the siren gave the "All Clear". Everyone cheered.

One of the teachers looked outside, then gave the signal to go. The children marched up the steps and into the playground. It had been exciting but they were glad it was over. It was good to move around and get warm again. But they could see far off a huge fire burning up a local factory ... a factory that Adam hadn't noticed was there before.

Adam was about to panic. He didn't like all this. Was he going mad? As soon as he could, he slipped away from the others and ran back into the hall. With shaking hands he pushed the iron key into the stock cupboard lock. He opened the door and flung himself in. This time he locked the door on the inside.

The light went out and he was in the dark. He counted slowly up to 50. Then he turned the key again and stepped out into the hall. What would he see?

All was well!

He cried out with relief. Everything was the same as it had been before he ever went into the cupboard. The dusty, brown curtain was there with all the clutter piled behind it. The flowery curtains were back at the windows and the Class 6 art display was up on the walls again. Even the hands of his watch had started to move.

Had some weird magic been at work? Or had he fallen asleep in there and was it all a dream? It had all been too weird to be real. He'd better put the key back on the teacher's desk and try to forget all about it.

He was just going to slip the key back into his pocket, when he felt something hanging down his back. It was a cardboard box on a length of string – the box with the gas mask that Jade had given him!

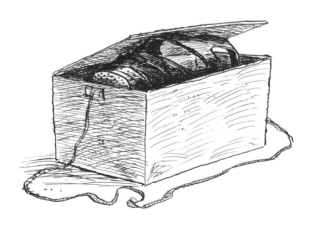

Chapter 3
Drastic Changes

Adam went back to Aunt Laura's and Uncle Tim's house where he had been staying for the last few weeks while both his parents were in hospital. Aunt Laura and Uncle Tim had been looking after him since his family had had an accident in their car. Adam had escaped with only a few cuts. But Dad had broken both his legs. Mum was not too bad but was being kept in hospital because she was going to have a baby soon and they needed to be sure she was all right.

Uncle Tim had told Adam that everything would be fine in the end. Adam would go back to his proper family. Until then he would just have to keep going and try not to worry. He mustn't mind having a different home and school for a while.

But Adam did worry. How badly were his parents hurt? No-one had told him exactly what had happened and so far no-one had let him visit them. Perhaps the unborn baby was hurt and he might never have the new brother or sister he'd been looking forward to. It might be selfish of him to think of himself, but he minded a lot that he'd had to leave behind all his friends, his school, the teachers he liked and most of his gear.

Adam's aunt and uncle tried to be kind. But they had no children of their own and

were not used to having a boy in the house. They treated him as if he were a small child. They were watching him all the time. He had to tell them when he went out and they sent him to bed much too early.
He couldn't talk things over with them as he could with his parents. So he felt very lonely and worried.

If he hadn't had the gas mask, he might have thought that he had imagined everything that had happened. But the gas mask was real. He had lifted it from the box and studied it in his bedroom. He had even tried it on. He hated the feeling of being closed-in. He hated the smell of rubber. How awful it must have been to have to wear the thing for real!

He longed to tell someone about how awful it had all been. But he could not bother his parents now and he didn't feel Aunt Laura and Uncle Tim would

understand. They would either say, "there, there!", or laugh at his weird story. If he showed them the gas mask, they might think he'd stolen it.

The only person who could help him at all was Jade Green. After all, she had been there with him. He decided to keep the key for a bit and ask Jade more about the secret room. Could he get her to come into the stock cupboard with him?

Adam slept badly that night. But next morning, he couldn't wait to go to school. He knew where Jade lived and planned to walk past her house. All at once she was there, in her neat school uniform. She was just crossing the street in front of him. But her friend Sophie was with her and the two of them were chatting away together. Adam was too shy to say anything to Jade.

It was only at lunch time that he found Jade alone. Then he showed her the key and asked if she had ever been inside the cupboard. When she said no, Adam didn't believe her. After all, she'd met him in the strange school hall yesterday and gone to the air-raid shelters with him.

"What about the secret room, then?" he asked her.

Jade laughed. "Oh, that? Well, let's say it's just a bit of gossip."

"All right then, what about the gas mask you gave me? Where did that come from?"

"Gas mask? I don't know what you're talking about."

"Yes, you do – I've got it here. It's in my bag. I couldn't leave it at my aunt's in case she found it."

Jade stared at Adam. What was he going on about?

"You must have mixed me up with someone else. I've never given you anything."

"Look, there's no need to pretend. I'm not going to tell a teacher or anything – we're in this together. I'm just trying hard to sort it all out and you're not making it easy for me. If I show you the gas mask …"

Adam began to open his school bag, but Jade turned away. She wouldn't even look.

"I don't tell lies!" she snapped. "And I wouldn't give a present to anyone who thought I did." Jade tossed her head and went off to find Sophie.

Now Adam was really upset. If Jade would not help him, he would never be able to solve the puzzle. He thought about his problem all afternoon. In the end he knew what to do. He would say nothing more to anyone. He would hide the gas mask in the stock cupboard behind a pile of books and try to forget all about it. Nothing was worth all this worry. He had too many problems already.

Yet he soon found out that he was not going to be able to get rid of his problem just like that.

Chapter 4
The Silver Monster

Next day, Adam hid again in the toilets after school. Then he crept into the hall when everyone but Mrs Yates had gone.

By this time he couldn't wait to get rid of the gas mask. All day it had been a worry to him. He felt as if he were carrying a ticking bomb around in his bag. And he had these weird fears that he was mixed up in something evil, like a wizard's magic spell.

With a shaking hand he unlocked the cupboard door and stepped inside. Again the light came on. Adam took care to leave the door open.

First he moved a pile of books to one side. Then he lifted the gas mask from his bag and pushed it into the gap he had made. He put some books in front of it.

As he stepped back to make sure the box was well hidden, his foot knocked the edge of the door. Before he could do anything to stop it, the door slammed shut behind him, just as it had done the day before.

Adam hadn't panicked last time, because he knew he had the key safely in his hand. But this time, although he still had the key, he was deeply afraid. The thing he feared most had happened. Now he had to do something about his problem after all. What would he find when he opened that door again?

Well, he had to open it. He couldn't stay here in the dark all night. And Aunt Laura had said she would take him to the hospital that evening to see his parents for the first time since the accident. This was a very important event. He had waited a long time for this. He wasn't going to miss it now.

Adam gave the door a push to see if it would open but it was locked. He had to use the key. He stepped out in terror. He was afraid to look around him.

His most awful fears had come true. He was back in the mystery hall again, with the two old posters and the black-out curtains.

Adam felt sick. He slumped to the floor and sat there with his back against the wall. He didn't dare to move. Then, all at once, there was Jade Green again, walking towards him in her shabby dress and cardigan. This time she wasn't carrying a gas mask.

"Do you want to come and see the barrage balloon?" she asked. "I know we're not allowed to go there, but we can hide behind the bushes at the edge of the field. They've got it on the ground today, which is something that doesn't happen often."

Adam sat there, staring at her. He felt stupid. "What's going on?" he asked. "I wish someone would just tell me what's going on."

Jade laughed. "War's going on, silly! But that doesn't mean we can't have a bit of fun. Come on!"

She held out her arms and dragged Adam to his feet.

Adam was pleased to see Jade again. Now he was no longer alone in this strange world. Nothing really bad could happen if the two of them stayed together. So he followed her across the playground and onto the football pitch. One end of it had become a vegetable garden with neat rows of cabbages, carrots and potatoes. How odd! The goalpost was gone and in its place was a huge notice saying in bold, red letters:

MINISTRY OF DEFENCE. AIR FORCE PERSONNEL ONLY BEYOND THIS POINT. TRESPASSERS WILL BE ARRESTED.

There were only fields behind the notice. Far away Adam could see a group of huts, with men in light blue uniforms moving around a great, silver monster which seemed to be tied to the ground with ropes.

"Look at that!" cried Jade. She sounded excited. "Isn't she a beauty? And it's our lucky day. They've taken her down for repair, so we'll be able to see her properly."

"So that's a barrage balloon?" Adam had to admit it was a wonderful sight.

"What did you *think* it was? Come on, we can get much closer if we slip through this hedge."

"But there's barbed wire."

"It's not so bad down here. We can crawl underneath it. Just keep your head down and be careful."

"But it says 'trespassers will be arrested'."

"Only if they catch us. Anyway, that means grown-ups like German spies. No-one's going to bother about kids like us.

We're finding out and learning things. They should be pleased with us."

Adam didn't want to lose sight of Jade, so he did what she said.

The children managed to slip safely under the hedge. They ran across two fields. They were just creeping along one side of the metal fence around the balloon site when the air-raid siren went off.

Chapter 5
Casualty!

This time they were caught in the open. Jade knew that the school's air-raid shelters were a long way off. All the same, she started to run across the fields towards them. She didn't care now whether she was seen or not.

"Come on! We've got to get to the shelters quick!" she called to Adam.

"Can't we use those huts instead?"

"Don't be stupid! They'd be really angry with us!"

"You said they wouldn't mind because we're only kids."

"Oh, shut up! Just follow me!"

Adam panted after her. What else could he do? But he wasn't looking where he was going. His foot stuck in a hole and he crashed to the ground.

Now he was really scared. He called after Jade, but she didn't hear him. She just kept on running. Adam got to his feet. His ankle hurt, but he decided it wasn't too bad. He was just about to move off again when a plane zoomed in.

It made an awful noise as it swooped low over the fields. It was so low that Adam could see the pilot's head in a black helmet and goggles, looking down from the cockpit. Then the plane flew up again and something dark dropped towards the ground.

A bomb?

The bomb exploded like thunder as it hit the ground. A shower of earth, stones, bushes and even a whole tree were flung into the air. A huge hole opened up and the next field vanished into it.

Adam had thrown himself to the ground. Something hit him on the side of the head. He heard an awful scream from somewhere in front of him. He looked up in terror. He was just in time to see Jade Green's body tossed into the air before it fell like a limp rag doll into the huge hole the bomb had made. Then it lay still.

Chapter 6
Missing Person

Adam Belman opened his eyes. He was in a hospital bed and a nurse was bending over him.

"I think he's awake now," she was telling someone. Then she began to explain to Adam where he was.

"You're going to be fine," she told him in a gentle voice.

Adam moved his legs and arms one by one. Everything seemed to be there, but he had a thumping pain in his head and he couldn't see very well.

He couldn't remember anything. That was bad. What had happened? He tried to think back and then remembered the air raid. He must have been hurt. All at once he could see that huge hole in the ground opening in front of him and Jade Green being thrown into the air before falling into it.

He turned his head and asked the nurse, "Is Jade all right?"

"Jade?"

"Jade Green, the girl who was with me."

"No-one was with you, dear, as far as I know. But your auntie's on the way, so perhaps she can sort it out for you."

When Aunt Laura came she began to explain what had happened.

"Don't you remember, dear? Mrs Yates, the school caretaker, locked you in the stock cupboard. She didn't know you were there, of course.

"When you didn't come home, I rang the school and they searched around until they found you. You had blacked out. The doctor says it's nothing to worry about. It may even be something to do with your car accident, or you may have banged your head on one of the shelves in there. There's a bump on the side of your head."

"I was hit by a stone or a rock," said Adam.

Aunt Laura looked puzzled. "Well, never mind, dear! It's all over now. They want to keep you in hospital for one more night to

make sure you're all right, then with luck you can come home."

"She's dead, isn't she?" asked Adam.

Aunt Laura looked worried. "No-one's dead, dear, and you're going to be fine. You don't know it yet, but you're in the same hospital as your mum and dad. So your mum will come and see you soon and before you go home you'll be able to visit your dad in the ward next door. Won't that be great?"

"But what about the air raid? Why will no-one talk about it?"

"Air raid?" It was clear that Aunt Laura didn't know what Adam was talking about. She was growing more and more worried.

"It was awful, Aunt Laura! But what I really want to know is whether Jade's all right. Maybe there's a different ward for girls. Could you find out for me, please? It's very important," Adam told her.

"Don't you worry about anyone," Aunt Laura replied. "Just think about getting better yourself."

Adam tried to sit up. "But don't you see? I can't get better until I know what's happened to Jade. She was hurt much worse than I was."

As far as Aunt Laura knew, no-one else had been hurt. Just Adam. The boy's mind must be confused. However, she could see that it was important to soothe him, even if she had to pretend to believe his story.

She asked first the nurse, and then the doctor, what to do. They told her to ring the school to ask about this Jade person.

"He's got this girl on his mind," said the doctor. "Once he knows she's all right and not hurt in any way, perhaps he'll settle down."

Aunt Laura did not look very happy. She agreed to make the call, but in an odd way she felt rather afraid of what she might find out.

Chapter 7
Jade the Third

Aunt Laura rang the school at once. As a result, Jade Green herself walked into the ward a little while later. Adam's uncle was with her. Jade was carrying a huge bunch of flowers.

Adam sat up in bed, looking better already.

"Are you OK then?" he asked Jade. He was amazed. He had thought she was dead or badly hurt.

Jade looked just as puzzled as everyone else. "I'm sorry about what happened to you," she told Adam. "Here are some flowers and I hope you get better soon. But I don't see where I fit into all this. I'm here because your uncle told me you were worried about me being hurt, but as you can see, I'm fine."

"Don't you remember the air raid?" asked Adam.

Jade's face lit up. Now she knew what Adam was talking about. "You mean the air raid Mr Evans was telling us about in class? You must have been thinking about my grandad's sister!" she said.

Jade started to explain to the grown-ups what she had told everyone about her great-aunt during a lesson about the Second World War.

"She was called Jade Green, like me. I was named after her and I even look like she did at my age. Mr Evans was telling us about this air raid that happened during the Second World War near our school. I said that was when my great-aunt had been killed. Mr Evans asked if it would upset me to talk about it, but I said no. So I stood up in class and described what had happened, the way my grandad has often told it to me.

"On the day of the raid, when the siren sounded, all the other children had been marched into the shelters. But Great-Aunt Jade had gone off somewhere on her own. She'd said she wanted to get a closer look at the barrage balloon which was kept in some fields behind the school."

"I know! I saw her – I was there!" shouted Adam.

"Don't be stupid – you couldn't have been there!" laughed Jade. "This was way back in 1942. I expect that knock on your head confused you. You got mixed up with what you'd heard in class."

"Now, that's where you're wrong," cried Adam, "because the gas mask was real! The one you gave me, remember? I even tried it on!"

He so much wanted to make everyone believe him.

Jade gave a sad little smile.

"Oh yes, I told you about the gas mask, too. Great-Aunt Jade left hers behind in school that day, something the children were told never to do. The school kept it in memory of her. I believe it's still around on a shelf at the back of the stock cupboard."

Slowly, very slowly, Adam began putting together the bits of this weird story.
He was still trying to make some sense of it when something else amazing happened.

A woman had just walked into the ward carrying a small white bundle.

"Mum!" cried Adam and almost jumped out of bed.

Adam's mum handed the bundle to Aunt Laura, then ran to hug her son.

"Oh, Adam, it's so good to see you! And Dad's going to zoom along to visit you in his wheelchair soon. He's almost better now. He'll be walking again in a week or so."

They hugged each other as if they would never let go. But at last Adam's mum took her bundle from Aunt Laura and held it out to Adam.

"Meet your new little sister," she said proudly.

Adam stared down at the tiny face and the tiny fingers. And all at once the problems and secrets of the past didn't seem important any more. Now there was this wonderful new hope for the future.

"What shall we call her? Any ideas?"

"Let's call her Jade," cried Adam happily.

And that seemed to please everyone.

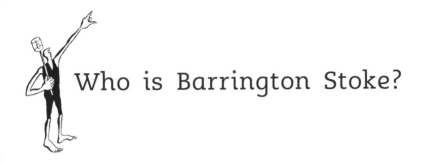

Who is Barrington Stoke?

Barrington Stoke went from place to place with his lamp in his hand. Everywhere he went, he told stories to children. Some were happy, some were sad, some were funny and some were scary.

The children always wanted more. When it got dark, they had to go home to bed. They went to look for Barrington Stoke the next day, but he had gone.

The children never forgot the stories. They told them to each other and to their children and their grandchildren. You see, good stories are magic and they can live for ever.

If you loved this story, why don't you read ...

Resistance

by Ann Jungman

Do you ever disagree with your parents? Jan is ashamed when his Dutch father sides with the Germans during the Second World War. Only Elli is his friend. Can Jan find a way to help the Resistance?

4u2read.ok!

You can order this book directly from our website
www.barringtonstoke.co.uk

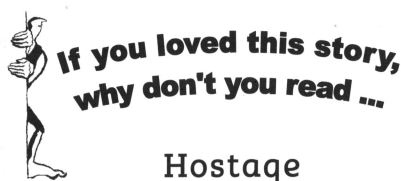

If you loved this story, why don't you read ...

Hostage

by Malorie Blackman

Can you imagine how frightened you would be if you were kidnapped? Angela is held to ransom and needs all her skill and bravery to survive.

4u2read.ok!

You can order this book directly from our website
www.barringtonstoke.co.uk